Acacia

Bonnie Vaughan

Acacia

ISBN: 978-0-578-39155-7

Published by Bonnie Vaughan, San Jose, CA 95136-2012.

Printed in the United States of America.

Cover art by Cedar Vaughan and Chris Vaughan, San Jose, California 95136-2012.

Luanna K. Leisure, Little White Feather Graphic Artist and Independent Publisher, Campbell, California 95008.

To order additional books go to: **http://www.LuLu.com, Amazon.com or Barnesandnoble.com**

Email: bonniegvaughan@yahoo.com

Contents

Dedication

This book is dedicated to my son Christopher Vaughan, who encouraged me to take authorship of my work and add my name to the cover of my books.

CHAPTER 1

"You've done it now, Caden."

Taryn sounded furious. Cade crouched with Nicholas behind a dwarf mulberry tree that shaded them from the artificial sunlight. Nick drooled on Cade's bare arm and pulled against the leash.

"Be still, boy," Cade whispered to his cocker spaniel. They'd get confined to his tiny room again if Taryn caught them.

"I know you're here," his sister said. "You and that awful dog have ruined my life. Dad wants you to come home now."

Her voice sounded closer. Simulated clouds floated across the fake blue sky above. When one of the clouds covered the huge light that passed for a sun, Cade crept through the shade to the next tree, pulling Nick behind him. The dog whined.

"There you are." Taryn ran toward them. "You have to come and pack now. Thanks to you, we have to move again."

Cade stood up slowly. Taryn's eyes looked red and damp. She'd been crying.

"Move where? Back to our old block?"

"No," she said, her voice fierce. "Nobody in this asteroid wants you or that dog anywhere near them. We have to leave."

"What do you mean, leave?" Fear clutched at Cade's chest. What had he done?

"Mom and Dad signed up for the Acacia Colony to keep you out of confinement. Because of you, I have to leave my new boyfriend."

Stunned, Cade rubbed the front of his shirt, where his muscles ached. He had tried to follow the rules, but there were so many of them, and some didn't make sense. Now he had gotten his family thrown out of their home again, like when they had to leave Earth to have a second child. Dad must be really disappointed in him.

"I'm sorry, Taryn," he said, his voice hoarse. "I didn't mean to cause trouble." Cade pulled Nick closer. "He needs room to run."

"You're allowed to let your dog run only in the community park, not on the roads. Why do you keep that big animal when we don't have room for him?"

"You know I've had him since he was a puppy. I can't just get rid of him."

"Well, you caused our neighbors to get rid of your family now. Come pack for the trip. The officials want us gone on the next ship."

CHAPTER 2

Cade stepped from the colony ship into Acacia's fresh air and bright sunlight. A class M star, Newbright, shined brilliantly overhead. Slices of two white moons hung in the air near the horizon.

The huge blue sky made him dizzy. He looked slowly around the landing site. Acacia trees lined a walkway from the gray spaceport to the outer edge of a giant green lawn. Beneath yellow blossoms, the tree leaves stenciled shadows on the ground. Cade sneezed.

Beyond the green grass, a eucalyptus grove waved its long branches. He hadn't seen so many trees since his family visited Earth seven years ago.

Nick pulled his leash to its limit. Cade jerked it back so he could wrap the end around his right wrist and grip the Kevlar cord in his hand. He couldn't let his dog run loose until they got to their assigned property. If he broke the rules here, his family might be exiled on a tiny asteroid with less room than they had on Bova.

"C'mon, Nick," Cade said as he pushed past Taryn.

"Quit shoving." She glared.

"Caden, wait," Mom called out, reaching toward him. "Let's stay together."

Excited people in line talked and laughed as they moved to make room for Cade and his dog to pass. He yelled back over his shoulder, "I'll meet you in the spaceport."

"Don't let go of the leash," Dad shouted.

Nick barked twice and jumped off the ramp, pulling Cade down. His boots landed hard on the planet's surface. It felt the same as the simulated gravity on Bova, as he had expected.

Next to Cade, the line of families waiting to go to their new homes reached from the spaceport entrance past the bottom of the ramp. The buzz of their conversations filled his ears. He would have time to run with Nick before his family checked in. The dog led him to the right, toward the grass.

"Stop!" A man in uniform held up his palms.

Cade pulled back hard on the leash, but Nick went through the gate. Sprinting to keep up, Cade followed. The dog barked as he ran across the lawn. The leash cord hurt Cade's hand, but he hung on.

When they reached a dirt path, Nick stopped, panting and drooling strings of spittle. A sign on a stick in the ground read "Dog Run." Cade dropped down and rolled on the lawn. He got tangled in the leash, which pulled Nick's head down and made him whine.

"I'll fix that," Cade said. "You shouldn't need to be tied up at a dog run. Dad would agree if he knew it was here."

He unclipped the cord from Nick's collar. The dog orbited him with a happy yelp.

4

Light from Newbright warmed Cade's arms and face. A breeze tickled his skin. He laughed.

"The air moves by itself, Nick, just like the vid said."

Nick yapped and hopped in circles. Then he took off on the dirt path. Cade ran on the grass beside him. Long eucalyptus leaves swayed in the wind, making the air smell like medicine. Cade slowed to a walk and stared at the trees, taller than any his parents had grown inside Bova. Nick sniffed the ground, lifted a hind leg to relieve himself on a tree trunk, and then resumed running back and forth on the path.

Tired, Cade lay down on his stomach and buried his face in the grass. It prickled his skin, its sweet smell mingling with the strong odor of soil. An ant started to climb across Cade's elbow when he heard his father's voice.

"Caden Li Martyn, come back here, now."

Cade got up but didn't see the dog anywhere. "Here, Nick," he called. "C'mon, boy." With the empty leash in his hand, he turned around in a circle.

Dad hurried over to the trees and asked, "Why did you let him loose?"

"I thought it was okay this far from the spaceport," Cade mumbled. He pointed at the "Dog Run" sign. A lump in his throat made it hard to talk. Dad was disappointed in him again. Cade looked at his boots.

"Caden, you know the rules. You're supposed to stay with us

and keep your dog on the leash until we reach our new home. When are you going to do what we tell you?"

"I'm sorry," Cade said, his eyes suddenly wet and blurry. He wanted to follow the rules here, but some of them didn't make sense. The lump moved to his chest.

"Okay." Dad patted his shoulder. "We'll talk about it later. Right now we have to find Nicholas and check in."

Cade followed Dad past the first stand of trees. Nick crouched there on his front paws, behind some low bushes, whining and wagging his tail.

"Must be some small animal in there," Dad said.

"What kind of animal?" Cade asked.

"Probably a rabbit. We have to hurry now. It's almost our turn to check in." Dad took off toward the spaceport platform.

"Nicholas, heel," Cade ordered, patting the side of his leg. The dog bounded toward him with his tongue hanging out. Cade fastened the leash to Nick's collar.

A brown, furry being shorter than Cade's knees walked out of the bushes on two feet and looked directly into his eyes. It didn't seem like any of the Earth animals he had studied. Cade saw intelligence in that gaze. The being stretched its arms, which ended in sharp claws, and burrowed into the ground.

"That's no animal," Cade said. He wondered how it could be here. Only this half of Acacia had been terraformed to be like Earth. The native Acacian animals, plants and trees lived on the other half, behind the barrier.

He jogged to catch up to Dad, with Nick trotting alongside, and thought about the being. It might have used its claws to dig under the barrier and get to this side. He couldn't wait to tell Dad. Humans were not supposed to terraform worlds that had intelligent life. Maybe the government had made a mistake.

Before Cade could get in line with his family, the tall man in uniform blocked his way. Cade looked up into the thin, tanned face of Governor Alex Druckmeyer. The stern gaze and steely eyes looked the same as in the governor's picture on SpaceNet.

"What were you doing out there?" Druckmeyer asked.

Cade held the leash at his back to keep Nick behind him, leaned around the gray uniform, and shouted, "Dad."

Druckmeyer stood straight as a launch tower, a foot taller than Cade. The man's black hair flowed back from his forehead to his shoulders.

"Well, what were you doing out there?" He tapped his boot. "Have you checked in at the spaceport yet?"

"No, sir. We wanted to stretch our legs first."

"We? What do you mean, we? Where are your parents?"

Cade stood on tiptoes to point over the governor's shoulder at Dad, who pushed toward them through the line of people and baggage moving in the opposite direction. Nick barked.

Druckmeyer stepped back and frowned at Cade. "You brought a dog to Acacia? Why?"

Without thinking, Cade muttered, "You're more annoying than my sister."

7

"What was that?"

"The vid said it was okay to bring pets," Cade said louder, trying not to glare into the man's tiny eyes. Cade reached behind his waist to pat the dog, who licked his hand. Dad had promised he could keep Nick.

"Okay?" Druckmeyer said. "Do you know how many rules you've broken with your dog, young man?"

"Three or four, I think." Cade dropped his gaze to the thick grass under his shoes. "Sorry."

Dad finally jumped down next to him.

"Uh, this is my father, Wendell Martyn."

With the right side of his upper lip raised in a sneer, the governor looked Dad up and down. "Please see that your son follows our rules. You signed the agreement before you arrived."

"We will, Governor Druckmeyer. He just hasn't seen this much room to run for years."

"I don't want to hear excuses, Mr. Martyn. For our colony to be successful, we need everyone to cooperate." The governor turned sharply on his left boot heel and strode away.

As soon as the governor left, Cade said, "I saw a native Acacian in the woods." As a biologist, Dad should know what to do.

"Not possible," Dad said. "This is the Earth-like side of Acacia."

"I know. It was small, with brown fur, but not like any of the Earth animals I studied," Cade said. "It walked out and looked at me, then burrowed into the ground with its claws. I think it might be intelligent. Should we tell the governor?"

"Not now, son." Dad frowned. "I'll check on it. Try to avoid Governor Druckmeyer for a while. We don't want to keep upsetting him." He smiled and pretended to punch Cade on the shoulder. "Let's catch up to Mom and Taryn and go home."

Cade went to their place in line and then shortened the leash to keep Nick close as they entered the spaceport. Mom handed their papers to a uniformed woman at the gate.

"About time," Taryn whispered. Her warm breath sprayed Cade's ear with tiny drops of moisture. "You should have left that stupid dog behind."

Cade wanted to tell her to shut up but decided against it. He wiped his ear, then clutched Nick's collar.

The officer said, "That's a fine dog, Caden, but you can't let him run around here. This is a controlled environment."

"I know," Cade said, turning away. Bova had been a controlled environment, too. Nick never got to run very much.

"We're sorry, ma'am," Dad said. "The boy hasn't been on a planet surface for seven years."

Cade had just turned seven when they visited Earth. That's where they found Nicholas at an animal shelter, a little, squirming puppy in a cage of dogs about to be destroyed to make room for more animals. Gazing out the window of the spaceport, Cade looked past the park and trees, at a line of dark mountains against the blue sky. Acacia was just as beautiful as Mom and Dad's native planet, with a lot more open space.

"Don't worry, Caden," the officer said. "Your dog will have room to run above your new house, just hours from here."

Cade nodded at her.

"Welcome to Acacia, Martyn family. You can take the next train to your new home." The officer smiled and handed Mom and Dad a paper. "This is information about our next colony meeting, in our amphitheater here a month from today. We hope you can all attend."

The Martyns boarded a magnetic train with the other colonists to finish their long journey. The train stopped over and over again to let people off along the way. Finally Cade and his family got off at a station where a land skimmer waited for them. They loaded their luggage into it, and Mom programmed the skimmer with the coordinates of their house. Along the way, Taryn pointed out plants and trees they hadn't seen since their Earth visit.

CHAPTER 3

Cade loved his new home on Acacia right away. He had a whole room to himself. The house was mostly underground, like their place inside the asteroid, but back there he couldn't play outside except in underground parks with simulated sunlight. Here he and Nicholas could roam about on the surface, under a bright sun, with no spacesuits.

They were exploring next to the creek behind the house when Nick started sniffing the ground. Wind ruffled the big spaniel's brown and white hair. Leaves rustled overhead as tree branches bent in the breeze. The dog sniffed underneath the pink flowers of a Baby Bear manzanita bush. Then, with his nose near the ground, he ran across the creek.

"Come back, Nick," Cade called. "We're not supposed to go over there."

Nick's hairy tail wagged as he disappeared over the top of a small hill. Where was the barrier?

"Nick, come back here right now."

Cade didn't want to break the rules again, so he turned and ran to his house for help. On the way, a yelp from Nick stopped him.

"Come here, boy," he called. The dog howled in response. Cade

11

ran back toward the noise and crossed the creek, hoping Nick wasn't injured. The vegetation abruptly changed to colorful Acacian plants and trees that he had learned about on the trip from Bova. He and Nick weren't supposed to be here. A force field should have stopped them. Dread exploded inside Cade as he realized that this violation could get his family expelled from the planet. Every step he took contaminated the biosystem, but his dog continued to howl.

As Cade climbed over the top of the hill, his shoes crunched on brown roga plants that covered the surface. He couldn't avoid squishing some of the maroon pods that dotted the plants. No bigger than his fingernails, the pods grew on vines that crisscrossed the ground like dirty plastic tubing. Blood-colored liquid squirted onto his pants, but he had read that it wasn't poisonous. How much damage was he doing to the native environment?

He spotted his dog tied by a green cord to the trunk of an ookwah tree, where large red leaves grew on fat branches in all directions. Who had tied Nick up? Nobody was supposed to live behind the creek.

The Martyns' land bordered the unsettled half of the planet, where no one could own property. Cade's heart thumped against his ribs, and his mouth went dry. He crept toward the tree, looking under the blue and yellow branches of every bush along the way. When he untied the cord from the trunk, the end slipped through his sweaty palms. Nick bounded away.

CHAPTER 4

The dog ran across a brown meadow between two stands of red ookwah trees. The green cord stuck out straight as a stick from Nick's collar as he circled back. Cade caught the end of the cord and wound it around his hand, where it stayed exactly as he put it.

"What's this green stuff?" he said. It felt like a huge rubber band.

Nick leaped toward some bushes, yipping in a high voice. The cord unwound and slipped through Cade's fingers. Instead of dragging, it stuck out in the air again.

Nick lowered his body and pawed through thick maki bushes, which looked like splashes of yellow paint on the brown roga plants. Cade followed, jamming his elbows into the ground to crawl under the branches. He tasted dirt and spat it out. Leafy twigs scratched him through the long sleeves of his shirt. He wondered if the plants were poisonous to dogs or humans. They had to leave fast.

"You're coming with me, right now," He told the spaniel, whose tangled hair picked up yellow burrs from the bushes. Nicholas whined and started nosing down a hole.

"No," Cade shouted.

He kept trying to grab Nick's hind legs, choking on dust that the paws kicked up, but the dog moved too fast. Cade dove down the hole. The cord dropped out of sight before he could grab it.

He went after Nick head first, closing his eyes to keep out the grit. Dirt filled his nose as he slid down the burrow. He dragged cool air in through the sides of his mouth. His shirt rode up to his chest, and the hard ground scraped his belly. The rough sides of the hole formed a tunnel just wide enough for him to move through fast, banging his elbows and knees. While he twisted and turned with the tunnel in his downward slide, Nick yelped in fear ahead of him.

Finally the sliding stopped, and Cade landed on his back against a hard, cold surface, with a thump that knocked the air out of his lungs. Eyes still closed, he coughed up some dirt and felt around his legs. Where was he? Did anything live down here? His hand closed on fur. He sat up but didn't want to look. Nick whined next to him and licked his hand. Sighing in relief, Cade reached over to pat the dog's head.

"It's OK, boy. We're all right."

Something rustled near them. Cade jumped to his feet, goose bumps rising on his arms. He rubbed his dirty hands against the inside of his shirt, wiped dust from his eyes, and then looked around a huge cavern.

Points of light studded the walls. Brown furry beings less than half his size surrounded him and Nick. Dozens of large gray eyes stared at them. The beings looked like the one Nick had found under the bush near the spaceport, but they wore green clothes.

"What?" Cade said. "There aren't supposed to be any people here." His voice echoed "...here...here...here.'

The beings scurried away. Some hid behind boulders. Others ran through dark openings at the edge of the cave.

"Where are you going?" he asked, with another echo repeating "going." Sweat dripped off his forehead. "I won't hurt you (…you…you…you)."

One of the furry people stepped out from behind a rock. Dressed in a green tunic and hat and brown boots, like a hero in an Interworld net game, the little being walked slowly toward Cade. It stopped a few feet in front of him and held out a four-clawed hand, palm up.

"Hello, Caden Martyn," it said in a high-pitched, metallic voice. "My name is Will." Dark eyes that wrapped halfway around the fuzzy face seemed to hypnotize Cade.

"Uh, hello," he said, reaching out to shake the claw.

Nick growled.

Will waved his hand in a circle. The dog stopped growling and wagged his tail. Cade didn't know what to do, so he just stood there.

"I would like to welcome you to our home," Will said, "but you are not supposed to be here. You must leave."

Will snapped his fingers. The loose end of the cord rose up into his hand. He tugged the cord gently, and Nick wiggled to his side, where the dog whined in pleasure and licked the furry palm. Walking away, the being looked over its shoulder at Cade and motioned toward an opening in the wall with its free claw.

"Wait!" Cade yelled. "Where are you going with my dog?"

Will stopped and turned around. A murmur rippled through the others, who crouched lower behind the rocks.

"In human years, Caden, you are not quite an adult. Your caretakers have told you not to go across the creek, and we cannot support disobedience in young ones."

"I thought Nick was hurt, so I had to follow him," Cade said.

"Young ones have many explanations and excuses, but it is still disobedience to the ones who care for you." Will turned away.

"How do you know my name?" Cade spoke quickly. "And why are you dressed like a character in a holo game?"

"My real name is too difficult for you to pronounce," Will said. "The clothes are to avoid frightening you. We must go, now."

Will left the cavern with Nick in tow.

Cade ran after them. "Come back, Nick. Here, boy." His dog didn't return. Bursting through the wall opening, Cade glimpsed the tip of the dog's tail as it vanished around a bend in a rock-lined corridor. Some glowing rocks lit the way.

Ignoring his sore belly, arms and legs, Cade raced after Nick. Furry things scurried out of his way, baring sharp teeth. Maybe dog meat was a delicacy on this planet. At least the beings seemed afraid of him, probably because he towered over them.

The corridor wound this way and that, climbing gradually. Barely keeping up with Nick's hindquarters, Cade fought to move his legs fast even though the constant, uphill trek made him want to rest.

"Would you just stop a minute?" he yelled at the strange being leading his dog away. The tunnel branched into other corridors. Cade had to save his breath to make sure he didn't fall behind, or he wouldn't know which way Nick turned.

The other end of the corridor began to look brighter, like they were heading toward a big light.

"Nick, where are you?" Cade sank to his knees, gasping to take in more air.

A bark came from the end of the tunnel. Groaning, Cade got to his feet and hurried outside. The little being stood next to a large awoxis tree, which had dark, blue leaves on branches that grew straight up. Holding the green leash, Will opened his lips to show pointed teeth. Nick sat on the ground next to him.

Cade showed his teeth. Will nodded. Maybe he was smiling, but the sharp choppers made him look angry. Will handed the end of the green cord to Cade and waved back across the creek, toward the Martyns' house.

"Uh, thanks," Cade said. "Sorry we bothered you. C'mon, Nick. I think he wants us to leave now." Cade walked a few feet toward home with the dog, then stopped and looked back.

The furry being nodded again, bared his teeth, and sped back into the corridor.

Cade looked at the blue tree and the rocks and bushes around it so he could remember the location of the opening. Then he jogged away, leading Nick home. He couldn't tell Mom or Dad about this because they might send Nick away. Maybe Taryn would know what to do. She was bossy, but she knew a lot.

CHAPTER 5

Scrambling down through the surface door of his house, Cade called out, "Taryn, help." At the bottom of the stairs, he doubled over to catch his breath as Nick dropped to the floor beside him.

"What's wrong?" his sister yelled. She rushed into the entry hall. Her purple sweats clashed with the red curls piled on top of her head.

Nick whined and started biting his paws.

"Are Mom and Dad still at work?" Cade asked.

"Yes, but not for long." Grinning, she added, "What did you do now?" She always enjoyed watching him get into trouble.

He undid the cord from Nick's collar while the dog slobbered on his arm. "Promise you won't tell?"

"That depends," she said. Nick pushed past her, crawled up on the couch, and settled down for a nap. "How did his hair get so messed up?"

Cade sat next to Nick and started removing the yellow burrs. He almost decided not to tell Taryn about the tiny people. He'd broken the rules again. How could he tell Mom and Dad without upsetting them or getting restricted to the house for weeks? But he had to report that the colonists had taken over someone else's planet.

"You have to promise first," he tried again. His head hurt, and his elbows and knees burned. The scratches on his belly throbbed.

"Tell me what you did," she said, bringing her freckled face close to his. He smelled garlic.

"Promise," he shouted. Spit flew from his mouth onto her cheek.

She pulled back, wiping the moisture off with her sleeve. "All right. Stop spitting. I don't tattle, anyway."

That was true, in most cases. He blurted out, "The people...this planet has people."

"It can't have," Taryn said, lifting her chin like a queen chiding her subject. "You must have imagined them. Or you're trying to trick me into thinking we have to move again." Anger spread across her face in a red blush. She reached out and twisted his left ear. "Tell me the truth, Cade. Is this a joke?"

"Ouch. I saw them. Nick found them in the bushes."

"What bushes?"

"On the other side of the creek, down a hole. They live in an underground cave."

"They're probably just animals that you haven't seen before," she said. "What were you doing on the other side of the creek, and how did you get through the barrier? Dad told you not to go there."

"Nicholas ran away. I tried to come get you, but he sounded hurt. The force field was down."

"It couldn't be. Where did you find the dog?"

"They tied him to a tree."

"Who? The natives?"

"Yes, with this cord." He showed her the weird, green material.

She took it from him, wound it up, and then straightened it out again. She dropped it to the floor, where the cord stayed straight. Looking at him closely, she asked, "Are you all right?"

"I'm really thirsty, and I hurt all over."

"I'll fix that. Then you're going to tell me what happened from the beginning, quickly, before Mom and Dad come home." She ran to the kitchen.

He put the burrs in his pocket, moved to the nearest chair, and watched Nick snooze. Taryn's sudden change in attitude made Cade jittery inside, like when he landed in the cavern. Was she really going to help, or was she just trying to get information she could use to make fun of him later? What could they do about the native inhabitants?

They couldn't talk to Governor Druckmeyer about them. The governor must know that they were there, because he had overseen construction of the colony. He might take Nick away or even banish the Martyns from Acacia for breaking their agreement. Remembering the governor's sneering face and beady eyes, Cade shuddered.

Taryn came back with a tall cup of lemonade in one hand and her pod in the other.

"No way," he said. "I'm not talking into that. You just want evidence to use against me."

She handed him the lemonade. The ice clinked as he drank the cool, sweet liquid halfway down.

"Have I ever told on you?" she asked.

"Only when I might get hurt if you didn't." He pulled his shirt down farther.

"Let me see your stomach." She took a tube of antibiotic cream out of her pocket.

"No." He put his cup on the floor and held his shirt down over the top of his pants with both hands.

She wrestled the shirt up, making his elbows hurt worse with the effort to resist her. "How'd you get those scrapes? Talk." She pressed the record button.

He sighed, leaned back, and spilled the whole story while she cleaned his wounds. He felt better after talking about what had happened. She turned off the recorder.

"Taryn, what can we do?" he asked. "We shouldn't live here."

"First, we can keep our mouths shut until I figure this out. I'm not moving again."

"We have to."

"Shut up until I finish. Second, you'll take me to the cavern tomorrow to meet these tiny people."

"What if they're dangerous? They have sharp teeth."

The upstairs door slammed. Mom's cheery voice called out, "Hello, this house."

"We're down here," Taryn said. She put a finger across her lips and glared at Cade.

CHAPTER 6

While Mom and Taryn fixed dinner, Cade waited in his room for Dad to come home, wondering how he could let the officials know about the tiny people without telling his parents. He should let them know first. Taryn would be mad at him, but she might even decide to tell because he and Nick had already gotten scraped up. Maybe Mom and Dad wouldn't notice that, though.

Dad's footsteps sounded on the stairs. "I smell something good," he said.

"Cade, come eat," Mom called out.

He walked slowly to the kitchen and stepped over Nick, who gobbled his food from a dish near the doorway.

As soon as they all sat around the table, Mom asked Cade, "Where did you get those scratches on your cheeks?"

"In some bushes outside," he said, looking down at a steaming bowl of split pea soup. He dipped a spoonful out of the bowl and sipped it, which made his face hurt. Then he looked up and tried to change the subject. "Yum, this is my favorite soup."

Taryn frowned.

"I want to take a closer look at you after we eat," Mom said.

"What bushes?" Dad asked, glancing up from his bowl.

"Uh, near the creek," Cade said.

Taryn's face turned as red as her curls while she ate her soup.

Mom looked at Taryn and then at Cade. His sister kept spooning soup into her mouth.

"What side of the creek?" Dad asked, his eyes locked on Cade's.

"It must have been this side," Cade said, looking down again, "because I'm not supposed to go on the other side." His face felt hot. He didn't like lying to his father.

"You two are hiding something," Mom said. "What happened?"

"Excuse me." Taryn stood up. "I forgot to turn off my curling rod." She left the table.

Mom stared at Cade and said, "Tell us."

"Nick found something in the bushes."

"What was he doing in the bushes on the other side the creek?" Dad asked.

"He ran across before I could stop him, and there was no barrier." Then Cade blurted out, "He found some tiny people in the bushes."

"That's impossible," Mom said. "He must have found some animals that are native to this planet. Stop telling stories to stay out of trouble, Caden." She got up and carried her dishes toward the kitchen. "Dad can decide your punishment this time. I'll be back with the medical kit to treat your wounds."

"But the people are real, Mom. They wear clothes." He hoped she wouldn't ask him to describe the clothes, which were straight out of a storybook. She went through the door, shaking her head.

"Enough," Dad said. "The advance team would have found intelligent Acacians, if there were any. Nobody would send colonists to a world that already has sentient beings."

"But they did," Cade said. "We have to do something to—? He stopped when he saw disappointment in Dad's eyes.

"That's not the issue, Cade. You went to the native side of the planet, where you're not supposed to be. Your presence there could compromise the ecosystem that was carefully isolated so we could live here without destroying the existing plant and animal life. If Governor Druckmeyer finds out, he'll send us away. I'm sorry, but you risked our home in spite of all our warnings. You can't go outside alone. I'll walk the dog when I'm home, and Taryn can when I'm not."

Cade had gotten himself into trouble again. His chest became as hollow as the Acacians' cavern. Restriction here would be like living inside the asteroid again. The walls around him seemed too close. "For how long?"

"I don't know yet. Until we're sure you won't get us sent away. Now go get yourself fixed up."

The hopeless look on Dad's face bothered Cade more than being restricted. He left as Dad started clearing the table.

CHAPTER 7

The next morning Cade heard Taryn's mean voice near his pillow.

"Wake up, you snitch. Mom and Dad just left for work. We have to go find your little friends."

"What?" Cade opened his eyes to see Taryn's face twisted in anger. Behind her, Nick barked and wagged his tail. The odd leash was sticking out from his collar again.

"Bring your dog," she said, turning toward his door.

"I can't go," he said as he jumped out of bed. "I'm grounded, remember?"

She turned back and glared at him. "You're allowed to go out with me, and you'll do what I tell you."

"No. I have to mind Mom and Dad, not you."

"They left me in charge," she said, reaching for his ear. "Now get your clothes on and let's go."

Cade sat fast to avoid her fingers. His scrapes and scratches still hurt all over. He didn't need more pain.

Taryn punched his shoulder. "Get up," she hissed, "or I'll dress you."

Nick barked at her and moved between them.

"Ouch. Okay," Cade said. "I'll get dressed, but I'm not going anywhere except the kitchen." He thought about returning her punch, but she could still beat him up. That would change soon, when he grew taller than her.

He pulled a jumpsuit on over his sleep shorts to cover his scratched up arms and legs, in case she made him go to the cave. While he looked for his shoes, she stomped out the door. Nicholas whined.

A few minutes later Taryn was waiting for him in the kitchen. She held out a cloth shoulder bag.

"I packed some food for you and the dog, so we can go now."

"Thanks, but I'll eat here."

He took Nick's kibble out of the bag and poured it into the dog dish on the floor, some of it landing on Nick's nose as the spaniel started eating, tail wagging. Then Cade pulled out a stool from the counter and crouched on it.

"You can eat on the way," Taryn said. Her fists balled up next to her sides.

He didn't want to fight. Maybe he could reason with her.

"Nick can't eat on the way," he said.

"So what? Dogs can go a long time without food."

"But if you run into trouble, he might be too weak from hunger to help you."

"What do you mean if I run into trouble?" She put her hand against the back of Cade's neck as he tried to eat a cereal bar. "I'm not going into a strange cave by myself. You're coming, too."

"You won't be by yourself with Nick along," he said. Her hand moved around his neck and squeezed his throat, making his voice raspy as he added, "If I go, you'll get grounded too for letting me cross the creek."

"I don't care," she said, leaning so close to him that her warm breath blew across his face. He smelled bananas. She released him and stood up. "Caden Martyn, you're coming with me. Now that you've told Mom and Dad, they'll investigate even if they don't believe you. Scientists investigate everything."

"Good," he said through a mouth full of orange slices. "Then maybe they'll tell someone we don't belong here."

"Not good. We're not moving again. I'm going to pound you if you don't come and help me fix this. Since you've already met these animals you claim are intelligent, they might be friendly to you."

Cade decided he didn't want to show Taryn where the little people lived until he was sure no one would hurt them. He jumped off the chair, away from her, and grabbed Nick's leash. At least Cade could outrun his sister now. As he headed toward the stairs, she tried to catch him but tripped over a chair. He looked back to make sure she wasn't hurt. Nick pushed around Cade and then pulled him up the rest of the stairs.

"Wait," she yelled from below him. "Where is the cave?"

CHAPTER 8

As soon as Cade stepped outside alone, he had broken the rules again. He wanted to do what Mom and Dad said, but he had to get away from Taryn. She would try to follow him. He pulled Nick toward a grove of holly trees to look for a hiding place.

"Caden, come back," Taryn called, her head sticking up from the house entrance.

He hurried into bushes under the trees to get out of sight, holding onto the leash as Nick squirmed in after him.

"Here, Nick." Taryn's voice sounded closer.

The dog yipped.

"Hush, boy," Cade whispered. Nick responded with a quieter yip.

"I heard your dog, Cade. You're going to be sorry you ran from me."

He clamped his right hand over Nick's mouth and scooted farther back. Cade's left hand touched the edge of a hole behind him. The dog shook his head back and forth until Cade let go of the drooling snout. He wiped his wet hand across his shirt.

Maybe he could lower himself into the hole, and Nick would

follow. Cade felt around the edges to find out if the hole was big enough. They would fit, one at a time, but he didn't know how deep it went.

"I'll find you." Taryn sounded so close that she must have reached the trees.

Cade backed slowly into the hole, holding a finger over his lips and making eye contact with Nick so the dog would be quiet. The hole slanted down enough to make Cade start sliding backwards. He tugged gently on the leash, and Nick started crawling after him, their noses almost touching. The cool underground smell mingled with foul canine breath. They slid down until Cade landed in a corridor of a cavern, like the one he had emerged from after meeting the little beings.

CHAPTER 9

Taryn would probably track Cade to the hole and follow. Before she found him, he needed to find the Acacians again so she would believe they exist. As soon as his feet touched the ground, he started jogging along the corridor, under the glow stones in the ceiling. Still on leash, Nick followed, panting. Soon Cade heard other footsteps.

Was it Taryn already, or were the Acacians nearby? The footsteps sounded in front of him as well as behind, as if he had an escort. He couldn't see very far because the tunnel twisted and turned so much. He looked back but saw only Nick, loping along at a slow pace. Why wasn't Nick trying to run ahead, as usual?

At the next bend of the wall, more footsteps joined the rhythms of running feet. Cade still didn't see anyone. As he approached a fork in the corridor, Nick yelped and pulled back on his leash. Cade stopped. Dozens of glowing eyes surrounded by fur blocked the path to his right. Tiny four-clawed hands motioned for him to go left.

"Thanks," he said. Maybe the footsteps were all from the little beings. Taryn might not find the hole he had slid down. He slowed to a walk as he took the left corridor.

The steps behind him increased to a slap-slap rhythm like a drumbeat. The Acacians who had pointed out the way must have followed. He looked back and saw a furry mass dotted with eyeballs behind Nick. How many of them lived down here, and where were they herding him and his dog?

He had to keep going. He couldn't return home until Mom and Dad got back from work, or Taryn would beat him up. She would find a way not to get in trouble for it, too. She always did.

Where else could he go? Would this corridor lead to the big cavern, and could he stay there for a while? At least he was probably safe from Taryn for now. If she had followed him, she would have already caught up.

CHAPTER 10

As Cade passed openings to side corridors, more Acacians joined his entourage, a few walking in front or beside him. They were taking him somewhere. He needed to talk to them.

"I'm Cade," he said, even though he didn't know if they could understand him. He stopped and turned to point at his dog. "That's Nick." The dog sat and thumped his tail against the dirt floor.

The Acacians halted, making squeaky noises. Was it their language? How could Cade ever understand it? He tried copying one of the high-pitched sounds. The little beings bared their teeth and seemed to snarl. Maybe he should just listen for a while.

He gave Nick's leash a gentle tug and started walking along the corridor again. Nick followed. Their furry companions moved with them.

When Cade started to pass the next opening, on the right, the Acacians motioned toward it. They rearranged themselves to block the corridor ahead.

"OK," he said. He took Nick through the opening. They entered a cavern smaller than the one Cade had landed in yesterday. He waited for his eyes to adjust to the darker place.

CHAPTER 11

"Welcome, Caden Martyn," a familiar metallic voice said.

Glowing rocks dotted the cave walls, like candles. In the dim light, Cade recognized Will, the Acacian who had led him out of the cavern yesterday. Across the back of his green tunic, Will carried a bow and quiver of arrows.

"How can you speak our language?" Cade asked. Nick whined and moved between him and the short being.

"I have a translator that helps me talk to you," the voice said. "No one else has one that speaks your language yet. We have been listening to your broadcasts a long time to develop this prototype."

"Wow," Cade said. "I'm talking to an alien." He shivered. "I mean, an Acacian."

"Ah. So your people have named us. We call you New Friends."

Cade laughed. Goosebumps covered his arms. "Will is not your name. He's a character in our SpaceNet games."

Will spread his tiny arms wide and bared his pointed teeth. "I'm trying to be friendly, by using a name that is familiar to you. You could not pronounce my real name without a mouth like mine."

"I could try," Cade said.

Will made a rumbling sound like a laugh and said, "Yesterday I could not be so friendly because I needed everyone's agreement first."

"Agreement?" Cade asked. "Aren't you their leader?"

"We don't have what you call a leader. If something I do affects someone else, I need their agreement before I can do it, or at least no objection from them. Being friends with you and your people affects everyone. We have been discussing this since I saw you last, and now everyone agrees. Please come to my place so we can talk some more."

"Lead the way," Cade said, pulling Nick to his side. The dog whined.

Will walked across the cavern. As Cade trailed behind, he smelled the dirt and an unfamiliar musky odor that made him uncomfortable. When they crossed a small, shallow stream, Nick barked. The sharp sound echoed around them. Glowing eyes in furry faces topped by green hats appeared from behind the rocks along their way. Squeaky sounds mingled with the stream's babble and Nick's anxious whining.

At the far wall, Will started through an opening, turned, and beckoned for Cade to follow. With Nick in tow, Cade entered a small, circular cave about the size of his bedroom. Large glow rocks lit the walls. A table with two chairs, the only furniture, stood in the center of the cave. Lumpy dark things that looked like pillows ringed the edges of the floor. One lump lay next to a chair and a rock that had been hollowed out to make a bowl. A liquid filled the rock.

The dog pulled Cade toward the clear liquid.

"Wait, Nick. I have to test it first."

"It is water from the stream next to your house," Will said.

Nick was already lapping up the water.

"From my house? How...?"

"We are everywhere."

"But I thought you were supposed to stay on this half of the planet."

"We did not agree to that. Are you staying on the other half of the planet?"

"Well, no."

CHAPTER 12

Guilt and emptiness filled Cade. He was disobeying Mom and Dad again and probably contaminating a delicate ecosystem. Were the Acacians contaminating the human side? But the entire planet belonged to the Acacians, so the humans should not have a side. He didn't belong here. He would stay just long enough to hear what Will wanted to tell him and then go home and face Taryn. He needed her help to convince their parents that they had to do something.

"Please sit," Will said. "Door 6531, up."

Cade sat in the chair next to Nick and watched a force field glimmer in the opening where they had entered. "How did you do that?"

"With what you would call voice-activated remote control."

"That number, 6531 – do you have thousands of cave rooms here?"

"We are everywhere," Will said again, pulling himself up into the other chair. His face just cleared the top of the table. "The man you call governor thinks we are only here, but none of us agreed to that."

"Why do you need to pretend that you are only here?" Cade asked, throwing his arms up and almost tipping his chair backwards.

"Why didn't you let the governor know you are intelligent so we would not colonize the planet? You must have seen in the broadcasts that we wouldn't take a planet that belongs to someone else."

"Food and drink, table 3, above and below," Will said. A small robot covered with containers came out of the rock wall and rolled over to Cade. It placed a stone plate with two cookies and a cup filled with a white liquid in front of him, a plate with green lumpy stuff in front of his host, and a bowl of Nick's favorite treats under the table.

"Did you take this milk, cookies, and dog food from my house?" Cade asked.

Will flinched as if someone had tried to hit him. "I would not do that, Cade. The items in your house do not belong to me. We replicated them."

Cade reached under the table and grabbed the bowl away from Nick. The dog growled.

"We can't feed him anything without testing it first," Cade said. "There are things we can't see that might get into the food and make him sick."

"I know." Will said. "That is why we replicated the food for you and your dog instead of preparing it. I am a biologist."

"Like my parents?" Cade put the bowl back under the table and bit into a chocolate cookie.

"Yes. I understand their work here is to balance the ecosystems. I also do this."

"I have contaminated your ecosystem," Cade said.

"Not just you. Your people moved in before they finished the force field that keeps the biology on the two sides of our planet separate. We had to do a lot of extra work to fix this. If they had asked us, they would not need a force field. We can keep everything separate and balanced if they want us to stay out of their way." Will's head disappeared under the table for a few seconds.

"It's not that they want you to stay away," Cade said. "They're afraid of getting sick from things they aren't used to, and they don't want to destroy your native species. They think you are animals."

"We are animals," Will said. "Yet we are intelligent enough to take care of our own planet. You are welcome here, but we do not like others telling us what to do."

"You don't tell anyone else what to do?" Cade drank the milk.

"Just children, enough to teach them and to keep them safe until they can decide everything for themselves. We do the same for our people who are forever children. We take care of them."

"Then why didn't you tell Governor Druckmeyer that you're intelligent?"

"He knows," Will said.

A chill ran down Cade's spine. The governor he had met at the spaceport took someone else's world. "Then why didn't you fight him and his crews to keep them from taking over half your planet?"

"Fight?"

"Yes." Cade got up and paced around the room as he talked.

"Why don't you get your weapons out and chase us humans off your world?"

"Weapons?"

As Cade walked in circles to control his anger at the governor, he wondered how intelligent Will was. "You know, war."

"Oh," Will said, "like in your games. Do your people really fight like that and hurt each other?"

"Not much anymore, but there were terrible wars in the past. Now people are supposed to fight only in the games, so no one gets hurt."

"We do not fight." Will stood up next to his chair. "We just try to agree."

"What if some of you don't agree?"

"If someone disagrees with me about something that would affect them, I won't do it. For something important to me, I would try to convince them to agree. I can be very convincing."

"Yes, I noticed." Cade stopped pacing and stood facing his host. "Then why didn't you try to convince the governor not to settle on your planet?"

"That's what I'm doing." Will reached out his furry arms toward Cade, his four-fingered palms up. "Caden Martyn, will you agree to help me convince your people not to force us to live on only half of our planet?"

"Yes," Cade said, "but I thought you wanted your planet back. Don't you want us to leave?"

"The planet is still here no matter where we live. Your people have altered the biology of half of it and tried to confine us and other native species to the other half without our agreement. We don't want you to leave, and we probably would have made room for you if someone had asked us. We just don't want your people to tell us what to do on our world. You are our guests, not our leaders. We have no leaders, but we understand that you do. So if we can convince your governor to agree, then maybe the rest of you will agree."

"I agree already," Cade said. "Can you come with me and meet my sister? We have to convince her first."

"Yes, my new friend Cade, I'll come with you." Will made the rumbling sound and bared his teeth again.

Cade laughed, too.

CHAPTER 13

When they got to Cade's house, he asked Will to wait in the entry hall at the top of the stairs. Then Cade removed Nick's leash and followed the dog as he ran down.

"Taryn," Cade yelled when he reached the bottom.

She charged through the kitchen door. "Now you're going to get it." She raised a fist. "Stop running in the house."

"Come upstairs."

"Why?" Her face reddened and twisted into a scowl. Her fist still threatened as she took a step toward him.

"Just come. Someone wants to meet you."

"You brought someone to our house?" Taryn screeched. "Without permission? Who is it?"

"You have to see for yourself. Come on."

He started up the stairs, turned, and waved for her to follow.

"Oh, all right." She stomped after him. "It better not be some boy, because I don't need a matchmaker."

Cade laughed and raced to the top, where the Acacian stood next to the front door, his head beneath the doorknob.

Taryn came up behind Cade and stopped on the last stair,

blinking. "What is that? Some animal you dressed up in one of your gamer costumes?"

"Taryn, this is Will, a native Acacian."

"You're really going to get it when Mom and Dad come home, Caden. It's illegal to bring an animal here from the other side. You'll destroy our ecosystem and get us sent off-planet. Take it—"

"I am pleased to meet you, Taryn Martyn," the metallic voice said.

Will's simple greeting left Taryn speechless, something Cade had never seen before. She stood there with her jaw moving but no sound coming out.

"The costume is supposed to make us more comfortable," Cade said. "They've been monitoring our broadcasts and picked up the Sherwood Forest style from a SpaceNet game."

She finally said, in a tiny voice, "P-please come in."

At the bottom of the stairs, Nick started barking, as if he suddenly remembered his guard dog duties.

Taryn led the way down to the living room and tripped over the dog. She tumbled to the floor. As she got up, she whispered to Cade, "How can he talk to us?"

"He's using a translator. That's why his voice sounds like a machine. It normally just makes squeaky sounds."

"We can learn each other's languages," Will said.
"Let's sit down and talk first," Taryn replied, back in charge of the house. She and Cade sat on the couch, which was too tall for Will.

She put a cushion on the floor, and he sat. Nick lay down next to the Acacian, the dog's tail thumping in steady beats on the floor.

"What are we going to do, Taryn? Thousands of Acacians have been relocated to caverns on the other side, against their will."

"We've always lived underground, where it's safer for us," Will said, "but before the humans came, we could choose where to live." He added, "There are millions of us, occupying many caverns."

Taryn shifted on the couch, as if she couldn't get comfortable. "Can I get you something to eat or drink?" she asked their guest. "You probably can't eat our food, though."

"No, thank you," Will said.

"They can make any food they want, and he just ate," Cade said. He didn't add that he and Nick had a snack as well. She would go ballistic if she knew the food hadn't been tested first. Cade waved his arms around and asked, "What are we going to do?"

Her eyes filled with tears. "We're going to have to leave," she said in a hoarse voice. Then she wiped the tears away on her sleeve.

"I'm sorry if I upset you, Taryn," Will said. He got up. "I should leave."

"No, please stay," Taryn said. "My brother told me about you yesterday, but I thought he was making up stories. We have taken over half of your planet."

Will sat down again.

"What are we going to do about it?" Cade asked.

"I don't know," Taryn said. "We can't tell Mom and Dad."

"Why not? We could introduce them to Will."

49

"We could convince them, but then they would have to report it to the government."

"So, isn't that good?" Cade asked.

"It is good to do what your parents tell you," Will said.

"I thought you Acacians didn't like to be told what to do," Cade replied.

"Yes, but I also said that we need to tell children what to do, to teach them and keep them safe. They can participate in agreements when they are adults."

"That sucks," Cade said. "Even in a society with no government, kids have to follow the rules."

"Your parents probably know what is best for you, Caden."

"Even if they do," Taryn said, "we can't tell them about your people yet. If they report that we have settled on a planet with intelligent life, the governor would probably make us leave and cover up the truth."

"Why would he do that?" Will asked.

"If he already knows about you," Cade said, "our government would take everything he has and send him to an asteroid because he let us move here. He might do anything to keep this quiet."

"Mom and Dad will be home soon," Taryn said.

"We can come up with a plan and meet Will at his caverns tomorrow," Cade said. "I know the way."

"It's against the rules for us to go to the other side of the planet," Taryn reminded him.

"Will shouldn't be confined to the other side," Cade replied, balling up his fists.

"But we are confined to this side," his sister said. "We shouldn't even be on this planet."

"You are welcome here," Will said.

"Can you come back tomorrow, Will?" Taryn asked. "Maybe by then we can think of a plan that won't get us sent away."

"Yes, and I can bring some of our engineers with me. They want to learn more about your communications devices."

CHAPTER 14

The next day Will arrived with two other furry beings soon after Mom and Dad left. Cade led the Acacians downstairs while Nick leaped around them and barked. Will introduced his companions, in his metallic communicator voice.

"Taryn and Caden, meet Chandra and Gregor," Will said. They wore green tunics and hats, like Will's, without the bow and arrows.

"Nice to meet you," Taryn said, "May I get all of you something to eat or drink?"

"No, thank you," Will said. "We have already eaten today."

"Hello," Cade said to the Acacians. Gregor was half a head shorter than Will, and Chandra's head just reached Gregor's shoulder.

"Hello," two more metallic voices said in unison. Gregor and Chandra bared their teeth.

Cade smiled back and said, "We don't really have a plan yet, but maybe you can help us think of one. The comm pods are in my room."

After Cade led the Acacians up his stairs and through his doorway, the dog crawled under the study table, whining and wagging his tail. Cade's room suddenly seemed too small, full of smelly canine and Acacian fur and Taryn's icky perfume. He climbed onto a chair and opened his overhead window so everyone could breathe better. Light from Newbright streamed in.

"Have a seat," Cade said. Chandra and Gregor looked at each other.

"He is inviting you to sit down," Will said.

They looked at the tall chairs pushed into the table and then at the floor.

"They're used to sitting on cushions," Will said.

Cade took the pillows off his bed and laid them out on the floor. The three Acacians sat on the pillows. Taryn plopped herself down on the brown plastic floor, crossed her ankles, and leaned her elbows on her knees.

After gathering some comm pods from his desk, Cade sat cross-legged next to Taryn. He spread the pods out in front of him, one for each Acacian. Then he and Taryn pulled their pods from their pockets.

"We type a message to someone like this," Cade said, pressing keys on his pod. "Or we can talk into it, and it will type for us. He typed "Hello, Taryn."

She turned her pod screen around to show Cade's typed message. Then she pressed a button. A voice said, "Hello, Taryn."

"Mind your parents, Caden," Will said into his pod. "Which button do I press to send this?"

Cade showed him and laughed as he played the message back. "You've got it," he said.

"I told you I was intelligent."

"Yes, but you didn't say you were a comedian."

The Acacians made the low rumbling sound. Cade and Taryn laughed with them.

"We have to be careful, though, about what we put in our messages," Taryn said. "The government can monitor them."

"Really?" Cade asked. "Now you're just being paranoid. Why would they want to waste their time listening to our messages?"

"Well, they could." Taryn stood up.

"I might have a plan, if you agree," Will said as he got up, his head next to Taryn's knee. "With your devices, we can probably make it work. Can you send the same message to all of your people here on our planet?"

"Yes," Cade said, pushing himself to his feet to turn on his wall screen. "I have a list of everyone here, and I can send a message to all of them at once. What's the plan?"

"We need to take the governor and his workers off the list," Taryn said, looking down at Will.

"We need everyone to agree."

"Some are not going to agree with anything that would cost them money."

"Why not?" Will asked

"If you do something for someone," Taryn said, "they pay you money, which can be electronic bits, pieces of paper, or coins made of rare substances. Then you can use the money to buy something from someone else." She pulled a coin from her pocket. "This is money."

"But why do you exchange this shiny bright circle?"

"Many people aren't going to give you anything for free," Cade said. "You have to give them something to get something."

"We don't have any money to give you for these devices," Gregor said, looking up, a comm pod in his claws. "We will have to return them."

"Those are different," Cade said. "They're gifts that I offered you. I can make more if I need them. What do you use to trade for work and things?"

"Nothing," Will said. "Everyone does work they want to do for each other and gives gifts to each other."

"What if you want something, and someone doesn't want to give it to you?" Taryn asked.

"It is our joy to give to each other," Chandra said. She held up her comm pod. "If you did not want to give me this device, then I would not take it."

"What's your plan?" Cade asked Will.

"Thank you for your gifts, Cade. Part of my plan is to use them to communicate with you. I can ask all my people if they want to meet your people. Then I can send you a message, if we have agreement, so you can send a message to all of your people about the meeting.

"That might work," Taryn said, "if you lose the green outfits.

Everyone in the colony is meeting at the amphitheater near the spaceport two weeks from today, at sunrise."

"Good," Will said. Then he asked, "Why would we not want to find our green outfits?"

"I mean, can you wear something else?" she said. "People will laugh at you for dressing like characters in a game, and they might think you're our pets."

The green clothes disappeared from all three Acacians, as well as Will's bow and arrow. They wore nothing but fur.

"What happened to your clothes?" Cade asked.

"The clothes were just holograms," Will said, "to put you at ease. We can come to your meeting dressed in appropriate clothing."

"What are pets?" Chandra asked.

"Like Nick." Cade said. The dog yipped and got up to lick his hand.

"You mean the animals you keep in bondage?" Gregor asked.

"I think Nick likes to be here with me," Cade replied. The dog licked his face.

"Tied up?" Will asked.

"For his safety when we go outside, kind of like a child," Cade replied.

"I understand." Will nodded. "He agreed to let me tie him to a tree so you could find him."

"You can talk to Nick?" Cade asked.

"Yes," Will said. "You talk to him."

"Yes, but I guess at what he's trying to tell me. I don't really know."

Nick padded over to Cade and settled down on the floor in front of him.

"I can help you with that later," Will said, "if you want me to."

Nick's tail thumped against the floor as he wagged it.

Cade leaned over to hug his dog and noticed that the engineers were taking the pods apart.

"They're going to break them," Cade said.

Will laughed with his rumble again. "Even you don't really believe we're intelligent. They are experts. If they take something apart, they can put it back together again. Then they can copy your device to make more."

"But they won't know how to connect to our data streams," Cade said.

"We have been connecting for many years," Will said. "That is why we can communicate with you through our translators now."

"Do your translators send a signal?" Taryn asked.

"Yes, to our data-collector banks at the caverns."

"Uh, oh," she said. "Maybe we should turn everything off."

"Why?" Will asked.

A loud knock sounded from the entry door. Cade's wall screen showed three uniformed officials waiting on the porch above the entrance.

CHAPTER 15

At the top of the main entry stairs, Cade stood next to Taryn as she argued with the officials. "These are friends of ours."

"They are animals," the woman in charge said, her hand on a weapon attached to her belt. "Let us take them out of here now or we will shoot them. No native species are allowed on this side of the planet. They are contaminating our ecosystem."

The Acacians huddled in a furry mass at the bottom of the stairs as Nick stood in front of them and barked constantly at the officials. Cade wondered if he should say anything about the Acacians being intelligent. It might spoil Will's plan. He looked downstairs.

Will shook his head back and forth, so Cade said nothing.

"Taryn and Caden Martyn, you are confined to your rooms until your parents return," the officer said. "We will wait here for them."

Cade started down to his room and waved to Will, Chandra and Gregor as he passed them. So did Taryn.

"Get isolation cages for these animals," the woman in charge told her officers, "and one for the dog."

"No," Cade said. He lunged for Nick, who kept barking in front of Will.

As the two officers went outside, Will gently pushed Cade back. Then Will's comm pod beeped behind him. When the official in charge turned her back to talk on her radio, Will checked the screen.

"All of my people have agreed to the plan," he said in a metallic voice so low that Cade could barely hear it. "If we cooperate now, the plan will work. We'll be at your meeting."

"OK," Cade whispered back. Then he said softly in Taryn's ear, "I'll knock on your wall after I send the message to the colonists."

She nodded, put a finger to her lips as she hid her pod, and then went to her room. Cade looked back at the Acacians as he went to his. How could all of Will's people agree so soon? Maybe it was a miscommunication.

CHAPTER 16

Soon Cade heard Mom and Dad discussing the Acacians with the officers in the other room.

"Your children have brought dangerous animals from the other side of the planet into your home," the woman in charge said. "We will keep them in isolation for a period of time and then return them to the other side. You and your family must stay in your home until the governor decides what to do."

When the officers left, Cade heard footsteps coming toward his room.

Dad swung his door open. "Cade, I'm very disappointed by your behavior."

"I know," Cade whispered. Heat rushed to his cheeks. He felt ashamed of his disobedience.

"We will probably be sent back to Bova," Dad said. "You got your sister in trouble too, and your mother is talking to her. We aren't even allowed to let you out of the house."

"I'm sorry," Cade said, "but it's not right. The Acacians are people."

"Give me all your computers and pods," Dad said. "You've been playing too many games. When this is resolved, we'll get you a good counselor."

"I don't need a counselor," Cade said. "I just need you to listen to me."

"I'm listening, but you're not making sense. Do you realize that your mother and I will lose the research projects we just started here, and we might not be able to find work again?"

As Cade collected his electronic equipment and handed it over, he told Dad, "I didn't know what else to do."

"Just do what we tell you. Is this all? I thought you had more."

"I gave some to the Acacians." Cade didn't take the pod out of his pocket. Sick inside, he realized he was being dishonest with his father again, but how could he send the message to the colonists without his last pod? When Dad got the message, he would understand, and they could talk about it. At the colony meeting, Dad and Mom would realize the Acacians are intelligent beings.

As soon as Dad closed the door, Cade's pod beeped. It was a message from Will. "Please tell all the humans we will be at the spaceport when Newbright first rises in the sky on the morning of your meeting." The officers must not have searched the Acacians because they thought the little beings were animals. Where had they hid the pods?

Taryn sobbed like her heart would break in the room next to Cade's. Why did trying to help someone have to hurt his family?

He sent an anonymous message to every human on the planet,

including the governor and other officials, who would hear about it anyway.

"The Acacians are intelligent. We have taken over half of their planet by mistake. They want to talk to all of us at the amphitheater when Newbright first rises in the sky on the morning of our colony meeting."

Then he knocked on Taryn's wall. Her crying stopped.

Cade's head hurt. His pillows were still on the floor where the Acacians had used them as cushions. He tried not to think about what would happen to Nick because it made his eyes sting. He didn't want to cry, so he rolled up a sweatshirt to use as a pillow, lay down, and closed his eyes for a nap.

CHAPTER 17

Cade woke up to the clatter of boots in the living room. A man's deep voice shouted, "Wendell, Rosa, Taryn and Caden Martyn, you are under arrest for sabotaging the well-being of the colony."

Cade jumped up and headed toward an opening in his wall that led to a tunnel with a ladder to the surface. The authorities must have tracked the signal from his pod, like Taryn said they would. A soldier banged his door open just as he jumped out.

"Stop," she said. "You can't escape. We have guards at all exits."

In the tunnel, he pulled out his pod and tapped a message to Will. "Sent the meeting message to everyone. We're all being arrested at home."

The soldier jumped into the tunnel, grabbed him under the arms with both hands, and hauled him back through the wall opening. Then she grabbed one side of his pod, but he hung on. Without it, he would have no way to contact Will. She drew her stun gun. Cade glared at her and let go.

CHAPTER 18

In a jail cell at the government offices with Nick, Cade sat on a bunk with his back turned to his family. No one talked to him. In the dim hall light, he saw movement in the next cell. Then he made out some furry heads.

"Will, Chandra and Gregor?"

"Hello, Caden," three metallic voices said in unison.

Nick whined and wagged his tail.

"Whom are you talking to?" Dad demanded.

"The Acacians are here," Cade said. Then he asked Will, "How are your people going to know about the meeting if you're in here? They don't have pods."

"What are you saying?" Mom asked. "Who's talking to you?"

"The Acacians," Cade repeated.

"We don't need pods," Will said.

"Then how can you communicate with your people?"

"All Acacians have a communications device in their brain. That's how we make agreements. All have agreed to the meeting with your people on the fourteenth rising of Newbright from today."

"What meeting?" Dad asked. "Caden, tell us what's going on right now."

"Please do as your father asks," Will said.

"Dad, meet our friends Will, Chandra and Gregor. They are native, intelligent inhabitants of Acacia."

Mom, Dad and Taryn walked over to the bars between the cells.

"Hi, guys." Taryn said. "Sorry you ended up here."

"Hello," Mom said, "I'm Rosa, Caden and Taryn's mother."

"And I'm Wendell, their father."

"Hello, Rosa and Wendell Martyn," three metallic voices said. "Nice to meet you."

"It would be nice if we weren't all in here," Dad said. "So it appears we have colonized your planet by mistake. I'm sure that as soon as the government finds out, we will all be leaving."

"Dad, Governor Druckmeyer knows about them and had them relocated to the other side of the planet against their will," Cade said. "He'll cover this up. We had a plan to stop him, by having everyone meet the Acacians at the colony meeting in two weeks, but now it won't work because we're in here."

"And we'll be lucky if they let us go back to Bova," Taryn said.

CHAPTER 19

A clank of metal made them all look up. The outer door opened. Then Governor Druckmeyer walked in. Ramrod straight and taller than everyone else in the room, he waved his cape for silence.

Nick growled. Cade attached Nick's leash to his collar and held the dog back.

"Mr. and Mrs. Martyn," Druckmeyer said.

"Yes." they replied in unison. Mom added, "We need to talk to you about the native inhabitants."

Nick barked at the governor and bared his teeth.

"I am here to tell you only one thing," Druckmeyer said. "Regulations require that I inform you personally. In two weeks you will be tried at the colony meeting, where you are sure to be found guilty of breaking our laws. Then you, your children, and that awful dog will be deported from Acacia."

Nick jumped up at the bars, barking. Cade pulled back on the leash.

"Your belongings will be packed by my staff and sent with you," Druckmeyer continued. He pointed at an older, short man carrying an electronic notebook. "My clerk here will stay to make the arrangements with you. Goodbye."

The governor turned on his left boot, his black cape swirling, and headed toward the door. Nick kept barking as Cade held him back.

"Wait," Dad said. "The Acacians that you moved to the other side of the planet are not animals. They are intelligent."

Governor Druckmeyer stopped and turned. "I told you, Mr. Martyn, that we have nothing more to discuss. If you persist in interfering with our official business, I will have you gagged. Please do not waste my clerk's time with nonsense. And shut that awful dog up."

The governor left, and the clerk introduced himself. "I'm Grady Hatstock. We have a few documents for you to fill out and sign." He held out a pod.

Nick lunged at him and hit the bars, growling again. Then he continues barking so loud it hurt Cade's ears.

"Mr. Hatstock," Mom said, "I'm Rosa Martyn. This is my husband Wendell and these are my children, Taryn and Caden. I'm not signing my name to any document until someone listens to us about these people whose planet we have stolen."

"I cannot discuss your radical theories. I'm just here to complete the necessary documents so you can depart."

"Then please leave," Dad said.

The clerk left without another word.

Finally Nick stopped barking.

Cade removed Nick's leash, turned to Will, and asked, "Why didn't you say something so they would know you're intelligent?"

"We tried that before, but they moved us anyway. If we had spoken now, they might have killed all of you to keep others from finding out."

"They wouldn't go that far," Taryn said.

"Tell them, Chandra," Will said.

"My partner, Patrick, tried to talk to the governor and Mr. Hatstock with the first translator prototype, so they would not relocate us. On the way home, Patrick got in a land-skimmer accident and died." Chandra made a squeaky sound, like a sob.

"Maybe it was just an accident," Taryn said.

"No. He was telling me that someone followed him from the governor's office. Then he was cut off."

"I'm so sorry for your loss, Chandra," Mom said.

"Thank you for your concern," Chandra said. "It's been difficult for my children not to have their father. I wouldn't want that to happen to yours."

"We just need to wait for Newbright rising in two weeks," Will said. "When all of our people see all of you at the amphitheater, we can fix this."

"How will we get out of here?" Cade asked.

"My people will come help," Will replied.

"Then how will we convince the other colonists that the governor knows the Acacians are intelligent?"

"Let's try to get some rest," Dad suggested.

Everyone climbed onto the cots except Cade. He wanted to find a way out of his cell. The Acacians might be killed if they tried to help him and his family escape. Starting near the floor, he felt along the wall quietly for some kind of opening. Nick crept along beside him.

Cade checked every brick as high as he could reach. Then he checked the bricks across the floor, one by one. In the back corner, under his cot, a brick wiggled. He took off this belt and dug the buckle under the brick to work it loose.

"Cade, what are you doing?" Dad asked. "I told you to get some rest."

"I found something," Cade said, "under a brick."

"What did you find?"

Cade pulled out what felt like a notebook. "I can't see. Does anyone have a light?"

"Here," Will said from the bars between the cells. His eyes glowed.

Cade held the notebook under Will's bright eyes and read out loud, "Evaluation of Acacia for Habitation, by Lisa Stronk."

"She was one of the scientists who died in the rocket accident before any colonists came here," Mom said.

Cade continued reading. "We cannot recommend starting a human colony on Acacia because it already has intelligent beings. Little Acacians covered in brown fur, with claws for hands, saved us from a wild beast.

"Three days ago, Newbright was setting as my husband, Rick Stronk, and I finished collecting our last plant samples in the foothills. We made a small fire to keep warm while we packed up our samples and gear. A huge wild beast the size of an elephant started circling us. Then it roared so loud I could feel the air vibrate.

"Suddenly dozens of Acacians surrounded us. They lit tree branches from the fire and held them up to scare away the beast. Then they used their claws to burrow into the ground and disappear.

"We had not seen these small beings before. They probably live underground to protect themselves from such beasts.

"As soon as we reported this to Governor Druckmeyer, Rick and I were arrested and held in these jail cells for several days. The governor told us that we'll be sent away from Acacia tomorrow. I'm leaving this notebook here because he'll probably have us searched before we board the ship. I don't think he will let us get away safely. If you find this, please give it to your council leaders. They will know what to do."

Cade felt stunned.

"You have proof now," Dad said.

"If the governor lets us get out of here alive," Cade said. "We have to leave now, Will."

"I know. I have already contacted my people. They are coming to rescue us."

Soon Cade heard scratching on the floor, and the bricks popped up in front of him. The same thing happened in the other cells.

"Hey," Taryn yelled.

"Shh," Mom said. "The guards will stop us."

Cade heard the lock turning in the main prison door.

"Come with us, quickly" Will said, "We can hide you in our

caverns until the meeting."

"Bring the notebook," Dad told Cade as guards began to rush into the room outside their cells.

Cade stashed the notebook inside his shirt and followed an Acacian down through the hole in his cell, into the ground, hoping everyone got out OK. The last thing he heard was a guard yelling, "What's going on in here?"

CHAPTER 20

Cade slid down through the ground again, following Will, through dirt that made him cough. He held Nick's leash tightly, with the dog behind him this time. Will dug through the ground ahead so fast it made Cade dizzy. He wondered if he would be able to make it all the way to Will's caverns. Then they turned upward, and Cade and Nick had to climb until they broke through the soil into Acacia's fresh air.

Three land skimmers waited for them and the other jailbreakers.

"The guards are going to follow us soon," Cade said.

"We'll turn off the lights and travel by radar," Will said. He nodded at the drivers, and the land skimmers disappeared.

"Where did they go?" Cade asked.

"They're still here," Will said, "wearing holograms that look like the surrounding trees. Climb aboard."

The land skimmers reappeared. Cade followed Will to the front skimmer while his family climbed into the second one. Acacians filled the last one.

They sped through the night, without lights, until they stopped next to the tree where Will had tied up Nick for Cade to find. The

Acacians turned on the skimmer lights so everyone could see to climb out. The sight of the tree made Cade feel safe.

"We can stay here until the colony meeting," Will said.

"But we have no food or clothes with us," Mom said.

"We can replicate food and everything else you need from your house."

"Druckmeyer will place guards there," Dad said.

"No problem," Will said. "As long as you don't mind if we enter through your floor."

"We don't mind," Dad said. "Thank you for rescuing us."

"Yes, thank you," Mom, Taryn, and Cade said.

Nick gave a happy yelp and ran to the tree.

They all walked to the cave entrance. Finally Cade would be able to show his parents the Acacian caverns.

CHAPTER 21

On the day of the colony meeting, while Newbright rose at dawn, Cade hid behind a tree and watched the colonists gather in the outdoor amphitheater near the spaceport. Most of them wore white tunics, the formal dress for colony meetings. A buzz of conversation stopped abruptly when Cade walked to a microphone on the stage in front of the crowd, wearing a white tunic over jeans the Acacians had replicated.

Soldiers ran up the three aisles that led to the stage.

"I invoke the right of an accused colonist to speak in self-defense," Cade said.

The soldiers stopped and looked at Governor Druckmeyer, who stood at the rear of the gathering, surrounded by security guards.

"Arrest him!" the governor shouted.

"He has the right to speak," someone shouted back. Many colonists stood up and moved into the aisles to block the soldiers.

"Thank you," Cade said.

"I've asked my parents and sister to bring some friends to meet you."

The Martyns rushed to join Cade, each dressed in striped jail clothes and carrying a backpack.

"Stop them," Druckmeyer yelled.

His security guards started pushing colonists with their nightsticks. Some colonists screamed and started to leave.

From the back of the amphitheater, Druckmeyer yelled through the sound system, "Everyone stay in your seats."

Will, Chandra and Gregor jumped out of the backpacks and stood beside Cade. They wore holograms of white tunics. The audience screams got louder.

"Silence," Druckmeyer shouted. "Stay in your seats."

The security guards reached the stage, brandishing their nightsticks and yelling, "You're all under arrest."

Cade held out the microphone, and Will grasped it with his right claw.

"Welcome neighbors," Will said, his metallic voice booming across the rows of humans. "It's nice to meet all of you at last."

Silence replaced the audience noise. Guards stopped in confusion on the stairs.

Chandra took the mike and said, "We hope you are enjoying your new homes." She handed the mike to Gregor.

"Actually, I don't need it," Gregor said, just as loud as her, as he handed the mike to Will. "I've already assimilated its function of voice amplification."

Cade saw Druckmeyer walk slowly backwards toward the exit and told Dad.

"Let him go, son," Dad whispered. "We can find him later."

The guards started retreating, and people sat again.

"Acacians, please come meet your new friends," Will said.

Suddenly a multitude of Acacians in white tunics filled and surrounded the amphitheater, as far as Cade could see. Druckmeyer could not get through the crowd. People screamed.

"Is this a trick?" a colony councilman asked from the front row.

Mom leaned over to take the mike from Will. "Speaking as a biologist," she said, "I think these native inhabitants of Acacia are intelligent."

The audience gasped.

Dad joined Mom and said, "Yes. We have colonized someone else's planet."

"How?" a councilwoman asked.

The Acacians motioned for Cade to speak. Dad handed him the mike.

"I have proof that the governor knew this planet has intelligent beings," he said as he pulled the notebook out of his shirt and held it over his head. "The brave scientist who wrote about them here, Lisa Stronk, and her husband Rick died in a spaceship explosion when Governor Druckmayer sent them away from Acacia."

The audience listened in stunned silence.

"I found this under a brick in my jail cell two weeks ago. At first the terraformers probably thought that my friends here were animals because all their technology is internalized. When they were being relocated to the other side of the planet, Chandra's husband, Patrick, came here to tell Governor Druckmeyer that they are intelligent. A land skimmer accident killed Patrick before he got home."

Cade pointed at the amphitheater exit. "By the way, the governor is headed for the spaceport."

Acacians gathered around Druckmeyer to block him, like they had blocked Cade in the cavern.

He invited the leader of the civilian council, Anne Rowling, to speak to the Acacians and handed her the notebook.

"We're very sorry we took half your planet," she said into the mike. "We don't belong here. I'm going home to pack. We'll set up a schedule to relocate all of you colonists as soon as possible. And guards, if you want to keep your jobs, please go get the governor and place him in custody."

"You don't have to leave," Will said, loud enough without the mike. "We want all of you to stay." He added, "Except the governor."

The audience laughed as the guards chased after Druckmeyer.

"We can live together here," Will said, "as long as no one forces us to do things we don't agree with, like moving to one side of our world."

The other six council members joined their leader on stage.

"We can't take advantage of you like that," Anne said to Will. "We have no way to compensate you. It took all of our resources to get here."

"You can teach us to fly through the stars," Gregor said.

The colonists cheered.

CHAPTER 22

Will spent the next few days teaching Cade how to communicate with Nick, while the Earth scientists taught Acacian engineers the secrets of space travel.

The governor was arrested and exiled from the planet, along with everyone on his staff who knew about the illegal relocation of the Acacians.

At next month's colony meeting, the Martyns and Nick arrived at the amphitheater after colonists and Acacians had filled it, side by side. Acacians covered the surrounding fields and hills as far as Cade could see. All the Acacians wore their green holograms of Sherwood Forest costumes.

Cade laughed and said to Taryn, "Will has an odd sense of humor." She grinned.

Everyone stood, clapped and cheered for the Martyns. Metallic voices punctuated human cries of "Hurrah." Will, Chandra and Gregor along with several more Acacians surrounded Cade to escort him up the center aisle to the stage.

As Cade walked to the microphone with his Acacian friends, Dad, Mom and Taryn stayed behind them. The council members stood on both sides of the stage. Cade motioned for Nick to sit at his side, as Will had taught him, and the dog obeyed. Then Cade smiled at the audience. Newbright beamed on his left in the early morning sky, while the two moons were setting on his right.

The audience cheer changed to "Cade, Cade, Cade, . . ."

"Thank you," he said into the microphone. Everyone stopped cheering and sat down to listen. "You have all helped me right the wrong we had done to the Acacians." Uncomfortable with all the attention, Cade looked at Will and continued. "Their very generous offer to let us stay has made them our friends forever. Would you like to say something, Will?"

"I always like to talk," Will said in the metallic voice of the translator. Everyone laughed. "Thank you, Cade, my human friend. I hope to get to know many more of you as we share our beautiful Acacia. Also, thanks to all of you for sharing your space technology with us, so we can travel to other worlds and make many more friends. Anne Rowling has something for you, Cade."

The council leader walked up to the microphone, carrying a large white envelope. Will, Chandra and Gregor stood next to Cade's left knee. His family stepped forward on his right. Will motioned at Nick, and the dog stood between Cade and Dad.

Cade felt nervous. He wanted to go run across the grass outside the amphitheater with Nick.

"Caden Martyn," the council leader said, "you are a hero of our colony. Acacia is the first world where humans and another intelligent species live side by side. Your fame will spread throughout the galaxy as you travel with this. We are honored to have you as one of our citizens."

She handed him the envelope with a smile. Everyone remained silent while he opened it. The document inside was a driver's license.

"This is a license to fly your own spaceship," Anne continued. "You can use it to help the Acacians learn how to fly to other worlds."

"Yes!" Cade grinned at her and the audience. "Thanks, everybody."

Will, Chandra and Gregor made squeaky noises beside him.

The council leader handed Dad the microphone.

"I'm proud of you, son," Dad said.

The words Cade had been longing to hear brought a huge smile to his face and moisture to his eyes. He couldn't speak, so he hugged Dad and let the rest of his family hug him, even Taryn.

"Everyone please come to the spaceport to celebrate," Anne said. Our new friends have prepared a welcome feast for all of us.

The Acacians made a path for Cade and Nick to leave the amphitheater, while the audience cheered. Then Cade ran with his dog across the huge lawn to the spaceport, as crowds of green-clad Acacians parted to let him through. Cade couldn't wait to show them how to use his new spaceship.

About the Author

Bonnie Vaughan became fascinated with space travel when the first lunar lander took off from the moon, a feat she had thought was impossible. As the author of numerous newspaper and magazine articles, her most exciting interview was with Colonel Al Worden, pilot of the Apollo 15 command module, who told her how fragile the Earth looked from a distance.

A journalism degree from San Jose State University landed her a job as a technical writer. While writing her own science fiction stories on weekends, she authored many software books for Silicon Valley companies. She is a "Distinguished Winner of STC's International Summit Awards Competition" and a member of the National League of American Pen Women.

Bonnie received some technical advice from Dr. Harrison Schmitt, the geologist who walked on the moon, for her novel Spaceborn, Published by Black Opal Books.

Spaceborn is available on Amazon.com. Her new book, Acacia is available on LuLu.com, Amazon.com, BarnsandNoble.com and other outlets.

www.ingramcontent.com/pod-product-compliance
Lightning Source LLC
Chambersburg PA
CBHW071415170626
46811CB00003B/1414